First Published in the United States 1998 by Little Tiger Press
N16 W23390 Stoneridge Drive, Waukesha, WI 53188
Originally published in Germany 1997 by
Baumhaus Verlag, Frankfurt
Text and illustrations © 1997 Klaus Baumgart
English text © 1998 Magi Publications
Library of Congress Cataloging-in-Publication Data
Baumgart, Klaus.
Don't be afraid, Tommy / Klaus Baumgart.
p.   cm.
Summary : Tommy, who is afraid of absolutely everything,
deals with his fears by teaching his new puppy how to face
all the things he himself is afraid of.
ISBN 1-888444-32-0 (hc)
[1. Fear—Fiction. 2. Dogs—Fiction.] I. Title.
PZ7. B3285Do 1998 [E]—dc21 97-51155 CIP AC
Printed in Belgium
First American Edition
1 3 5 7 9 10 8 6 4 2

Don't Be Afraid, Tommy

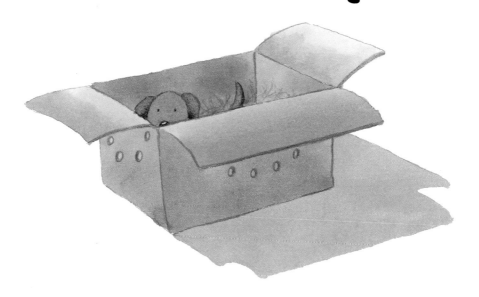

Klaus Baumgart

Little Tiger Press

Tommy was afraid of everything.

When it started to rain, he was afraid to put on his boots. He was sure there would be creepy crawlies in them.

He got a flashlight and peered into the toes of the boots. He found a stone, a bit of fluff, and a funny sort of smell. But he didn't find any creepy crawlies.

At the beach, Tommy was afraid of being chilly. The sun might go under and I might catch cold, he thought.

He got a big winter scarf and wound it around his neck. He caught a shell and a crab and a beach ball. But he didn't catch a cold.

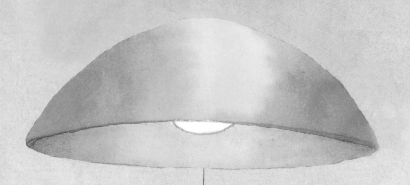

When Tommy came across
a spider, he was afraid of it, too.
It might attack me with its
long, wiggly legs, he thought.
He climbed up on his desk and
shook and shivered while the
spider dangled in front of him.
He knocked over a cup and
made a splotch on the carpet.
But he didn't get attacked by
the wild spider.

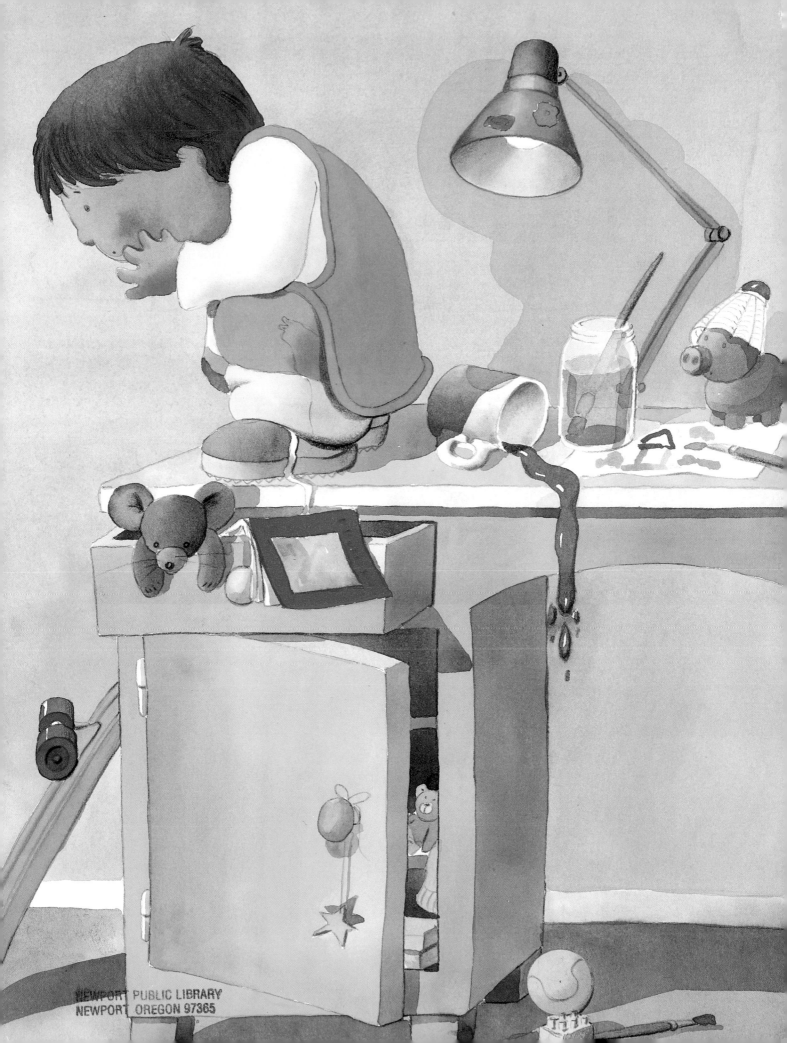

At night he sometimes told his mother how afraid he was. "You've got too much imagination," she would say before kissing him good night.

After she left, Tommy huddled under the blanket. He was sure he could hear strange monsters scratch and rattle the windows. Poor Tommy was too scared to go to sleep, and he was much too scared to get up and go into the bathroom. There might be an octopus hiding in the toilet. It was safer to use his potty instead.

But even an octopus didn't seem as bad as Aunt Martha. With her big slobbery kisses, she was almost the scariest thing of all!

Tommy was frightened of the bath. He was sure
he would get sucked down the drain. So he used his
mother's giant dishpan instead.

"I wonder what would make you feel braver," she
said one day.

"I don't know," Tommy whispered. And he crept
away to worry about that, too.

When Tommy's birthday
drew near, he was more worried
than ever. What if his party hat
got stuck on his head? What if all
the balloons popped? What if his
birthday cake made him sick?

When his mother gave him her present,
he was afraid to open it. What if it was a
snake or a lizard? Finally, he peeked inside.
It wasn't a snake or a lizard. And it wasn't
even the tiniest bit scary.

"A puppy!" he cried. "Thanks, Mom. I'm
going to call him Roly."

"It will be strange for him in a new house
with new people," she warned. "You'll have to
teach him not to be afraid."

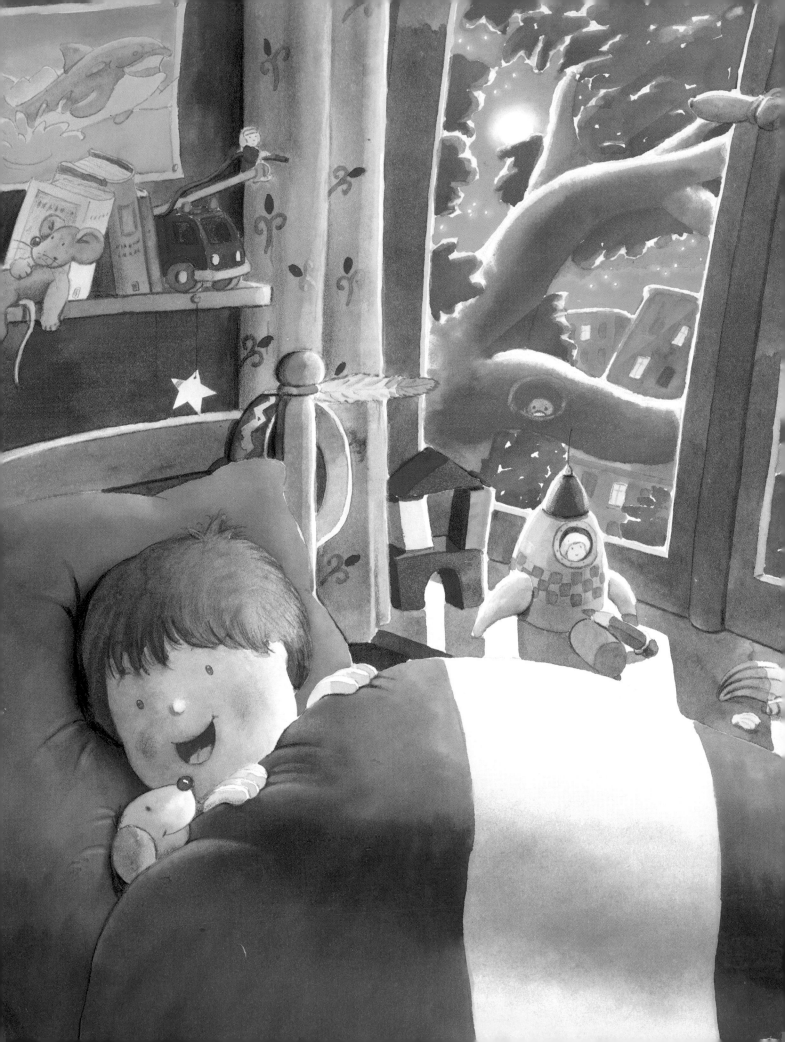

That night when Tommy tucked Roly into bed, he thought he felt the little dog tremble. Outside, the strange monsters scratched and moaned. Tommy pulled the puppy close. "Don't be afraid," he said bravely. "It's not really monsters. It's only the wind in the trees."

And later,
when he went to
the bathroom, he took
Roly with him, just in case
the puppy was scared to be left alone.

The next day Roly met the spider. "It won't hurt you," Tommy told him, making his voice sound big and strong. "It's just a little dot with long, wiggly legs."

At bath time, Tommy got into the tub and ran the water deep. He kicked and splashed and sprayed, and wild waves crashed over them both. Roly gazed up at him with trustful eyes. Tommy knew his puppy felt safe with him.

Every day Tommy watched
Roly get braver and braver.
He wriggled into Tommy's
boots to check the toes.

He even stayed when Aunt Martha
gave him a big slobbery kiss.

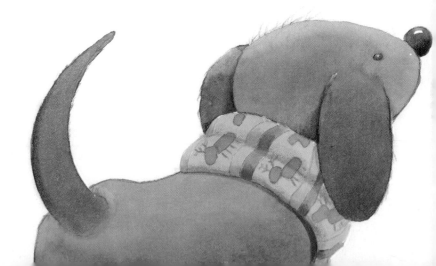

One day Tommy's mother asked him if he'd like to go for a walk. Tommy nodded happily. "As long as Roly can come, too," he said.

With his puppy rolling along behind him, Tommy thought that too much imagination wasn't such a bad thing after all. It helped make Roly seem like a real dog. And as he stepped into the street with Mom and Roly, Tommy didn't feel afraid at all.